D1052555

Look for other

titles:

# World's Weirdest Critters

# Creepy Stuff

# Odd-inary People

by Mary Packard

and the Editors of Ripley Entertainment Inc.

illustrations by Leanne Franson

SCHOLASTIC INC.

New York   Toronto   London   Auckland   Sydney
Mexico City   New Delhi   Hong Kong   Buenos Aires

Developed by Nancy Hall, Inc.
Designed by R studio T
Cover design by Atif Toor
Photo research by Laura Miller

If you purchased this book without a cover, you should be aware that this book is stolen property. It was reported as "unsold and destroyed" to the publisher, and neither the author nor the publisher has received any payment for this "stripped book."

Copyright © 2002 by Ripley Entertainment Inc.
All rights reserved. Ripley's Believe It or Not!, Believe It or Not!, and Believe It! are registered trademarks of Ripley Entertainment Inc. Published by Scholastic Inc. SCHOLASTIC and associated logos are trademarks and/or registered trademarks of Scholastic Inc.

No part of this work may be reproduced, stored in a retrieval system, or transmitted in any form or by any means, electronic, mechanical, photocopying, recording, or otherwise without written permission of the publisher. For information regarding permission, write to Scholastic Inc., Attention: Permissions Department, 555 Broadway, New York, NY 10012.

ISBN 0-439-31458-5

12  11  10  9  8  7  6  5  4  3  2  1        2  3  4  5  6  7 / 0

Printed in the U.S.A.
First Scholastic printing, February 2002

# Contents

# Odd-inary People

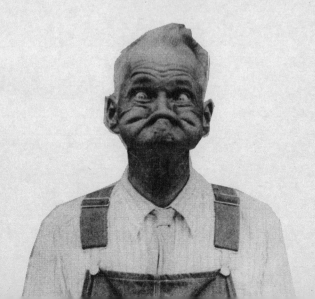

# Introduction

## The Odd-inary World of Robert Ripley

Robert Ripley was the first cartoonist in history to become a millionaire. The "Indiana Jones" of his time, he traveled all over the world, looking for amazing facts, oddities, and curiosities. Ripley delighted in learning about the customs of the people who lived in the countries he visited. When he returned home, he would often tell their stories in his Believe It or Not! cartoons.

An avid people watcher, Ripley captured his subjects in countless photographs. He was especially intrigued by those people whose physical appearance varied from the norm. Many of these human oddities appeared in person at Ripley's Odditoriums. Others were cast in wax and can still be seen in Odditoriums, museums of the fascinating and bizarre, all over the world.

Robert Ripley opened his first Odditorium at the 1933 Chicago World's Fair, A Century of Progress International Exposition. More than two million people passed through its doors, making it one of the most popular exhibits. People fainted at the sight of contortionists, magicians, eye-poppers, fireproof people,

and razor-blade eaters—but that did not stop them from coming back for more!

The first Odditorium was such a success that Ripley opened other Odditoriums in Cleveland, San Diego, Dallas, San Francisco, and New York. Like the first one, they were all hugely successful, featuring such people pleasers as vaudeville artists, contortionists, and odd-looking people of all shapes and sizes.

No one dared use the word "freak" in the presence of Robert Ripley. He had a deep regard for the unusual people who performed in his Odditoriums, and he expected everyone else to show them the same respect he did. Knowing that they would be treated well, performance artists flocked to Ripley's door from far and wide—a man who could swallow a mouse and cough it up unharmed from his stomach, a one-legged tap dancer, a man who could talk with his mouth full of billiard balls. There was even a man who could turn his head around 180 degrees and look directly behind himself.

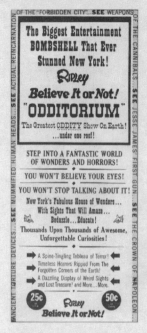

In the following pages you'll meet unusual people from all over the world. You can also test your "stranger than fiction" smarts by taking the Would You Believe? quizzes and solving the Brain Buster in each chapter. Then you can try the special Pop Quiz at the end of the book and use the scorecard to find out your Ripley's Rank.

So get ready to enter the world of men, women, and children from the past and present whose uniqueness is bound to amaze you.

# Believe It!®

**Some unusual-looking people are born with unique features, but others go to great lengths to achieve the bizarre look they want.**

**Omi, Oh, My!** An English military officer in World War I, the Great Omi sported tattoos from the top of his head to the bottom of his feet. It took 15 million needle stabs to do the job.

## Would You Believe?

An 18th-century Englishman named Thomas Wedders had a 7.5-inch long . . .

**a.** big toe.
**b.** nose.
**c.** earlobe.
**d.** little finger.

**Messie Hair:** French actor Pierre Messie could move his hair at will, causing it to stand, fall, or curl. He could even curl one side while leaving the other straight. What accounted for this ability? Messie may have had unusually well-developed muscles in his hair follicles. This trait is common in some animal species but is rare in human beings.

**On File:** In 1974, Renda Long of Glendale, Arizona, started growing her fingernails. By 1985, her longest nail had reached 14.5 inches while the shortest was a mere 8.5 inches.

**Hair to There:** One-time holder of the world's record, Lydia McPherson's red hair eventually grew to a length of seven feet four inches.

## Would You Believe?

In 1937 at the Cleveland Odditorium, Johnny Eck was billed as the "most remarkable man" alive because he was born with . . .

**a.** two noses.
**b.** hooves instead of feet.
**c.** only half a body.
**d.** a transparent body.

## Reptile Man:

Erik Sprague of Albany, New York, had himself tattooed with scales from head to toe. These, along with his surgically split tongue and the bony ridge that was set into his forehead, make him look like a reptile.

**Quadruple Pupil:** Liu Ch'ung of Shansi, China, was born in A.D. 955 with two pupils in each eye. His unusual

anatomy did not keep him from having a successful political career as governor of Shansi and minister of state. Ch'ung was one of Ripley's all-time favorite "human oddities" and is one of the most popular wax figures in a number of Ripley's Odditoriums.

**Bearded Wonder:** Edwin Smith, a miner during the mid-1800s California gold rush, liked his beard so much, he let it grow for 16 years. It reached a length of eight feet—so long that Smith had to hire a servant just to wash and comb it!

**Hairy Problem:** A rare condition called hypertrichosis, also known as "werewolf syndrome," causes uncontrolled hair growth. Jo Jo the Dog-Faced Boy, who suffered from the condition, was a popular circus performer in the 1880s. Today, brothers Larry and Danny Gomez, who live near Guadalajara, Mexico, have found a way to capitalize on their condition. They call themselves the Wolf Brothers and are known all over the world for their skill as trapeze artists.

## The Human Unicorn:
In 1928, Ripley found a photograph of a Manchurian farmer known only as Weng, who had a 13-inch horn on the back of his head.

**Lighting the Way:** In 1923, Ripley met a man in Chunking, China, who had a hole in his head. Known as Lighthouse Man, he made good use of the hole by sticking a candle into it (*see color insert*) and using the light to guide visitors around dark city streets.

**Left Again and Again:** Every male in the Colombière family of Nancy, France, was born with two left hands. The men were perfectly normal in every way except that both of their hands had thumbs on the right side.

## Would You Believe?
Pogonophobia is the scientific term for a fear of . . .

**a.** beards.
**b.** long fingernails.
**c.** tattoos.
**d.** red hair.

## Above It All:

Born in 1918, Robert Wadlow of Alton, Illinois, grew to a height of eight feet eleven inches. In order for him to ride in the family car, the front passenger seat had to be removed to allow room for his long legs. A kind and generous soul, Wadlow was dubbed "the gentle giant" by the people of his hometown.

**Tallboy:** Igor Ladan of Russia stood six feet tall when he was seven years old.

**Diaper Service:** During the French Revolution, Monsieur Richebourg, who at 21 was the size of a two-year-old, was a spy for the Royalists. He smuggled information through enemy lines by posing as a baby and concealing the messages in his diapers.

**Little Big Man:** Though he weighed a whopping nine pounds two ounces at birth, Tom Thumb never grew beyond three feet four inches tall. But that did not keep him from becoming one of the biggest celebrities of his time. In the 1860s, Thumb was received by the queens of England, France, Spain, and Belgium, and his fame helped him amass an immense fortune. He married Lavinia Warren in 1863 in a ceremony attended by dignitaries from all over the world. The reception featured a wedding cake that weighed 80 pounds—more than the bride and groom combined. The tiny couple settled in Connecticut, where they acquired a mansion filled with antique furniture—all miniaturized, of course.

## Would You Believe?

Colon T. Updike was known as "the human horse" because he had . . .

**a.** hair too thick to cut.
**b.** a taste for oats and hay.
**c.** a hairy 18-inch-long mane.
**d.** hooves.

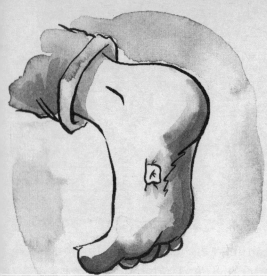

**Nothing but the Tooth:** In 1978, Doug Pritchard, age 13, of Lenoir, North Carolina, went to his doctor with a sore foot. The diagnosis? There was a tooth growing in the bottom of his instep!

**More to Love:** This baby, born in 1936, weighed 92 pounds at the age of six months.

**Big Foot:** In 1999, Nike made the first size 23 sneaker especially for Brad Millard of St. Mary's College in California. This is the largest size sneaker Nike has ever made—even larger than Shaquille O'Neal's, which is a mere size 22. Millard's basketball coach jokes, "When Brad gets a new pair of sneakers, I take the box home and use it as an extra bedroom."

**Tall Story:** Born in the mid-1800s, Anna Swan of Canada was as tall as her mother by the age of six. At 14, she was a foot taller than her father. She finally stopped growing at seven feet five and one-half inches. After a short career in P. T. Barnum's museum, Swan set sail for Europe. On the ship, she met and fell in love with Captain Martin Van Buren Bates of the Confederate cavalry. Just slightly shorter than Swan, the captain came from a long line of giants and was still growing at the age of 24. The couple married and settled in Ohio, where they built an 18-room house with 14-foot-high ceilings. All their furniture was giant-sized— even Anna's grand piano, which was mounted on three-foot stilts. In 1873, the couple had a baby boy, who weighed a strapping 23.5 pounds at birth.

## Would You Believe?

Adam Rainer, born in Austria in 1899, stood three feet ten inches when he was 21. Yet when he died at the age of 51, he was . . .

**a.** six feet ten inches.
**b.** three feet four inches.
**c.** seven feet eight inches.
**d.** five feet nine inches.

## Tooth or Dare:

During the Middle Ages, fashionable women in Japan blackened their teeth to make themselves attractive to others.

## Anatomically Incorrect:

Long-necked women are considered beautiful by the Padaung people of Myanmar (formerly Burma). To achieve this look, a female is fitted with a metal necklace in early childhood. More necklace rings are added as she grows until the neck has been stretched to the desired length. The catch? The rings must be worn for life.

**Queen of De Nile:** Elizabeth Christensen, 39-year-old wife and mother, believes she is the reincarnation of Queen Nefertiti, who lived over 3,000 years ago. Christensen has spent $250,000 on 240 operations to sculpt her face into a likeness of the Egyptian queen (*see color insert*).

**Lip Service:** In the past, women of the Sara people of Chad, Africa, tried to make themselves unattractive to slave raiders. In childhood, a girl's lips were pierced and wooden plates inserted. The size of the plates was gradually increased. Eventually, the lower lip was stretched enough that a 14-inch plate could be worn.

**Tri-lingual:** Edward Bovington was born in Burnham, England, in the 16th century with two eyes, one nose, and one mouth—but three tongues.

## Would You Believe?

For many years, every single person in Cervera de Buitrago, Spain, was born with . . .

**a.** two left feet.
**b.** only one eye.
**c.** no fingernails or toenails.
**d.** six fingers on each hand.

15

## Eggs-aggerated Headlines:

During the early 20th century, the Mangbetu people of Central Africa considered elongated skulls a sign of beauty and intelligence. To achieve this highly desirable shape, they bound the heads of infants. In adulthood, both men and women wore hats or wrapped their hair around baskets to make the head look even longer.

## Catwoman:

Socialite Jocelyne Wildenstein is also known as the "Bride of Wildenstein" because she's had so much plastic surgery. Why? Because she wanted to look like one of the cats in her billionaire husband's private jungle (*see color insert*).

## Would You Believe?

For a time during the reign of Louis XIV of France, it was the fashion to bind a young girl's head with laces in order to form long ridges in her scalp that could . . .

**a.** support the three-foot-tall hairstyles of the day.
**b.** hold hair jewels securely.
**c.** support many layers of braids.
**d.** securely hold several yards of ribbon.

# Brain Buster

The Ripley files are packed with info that's too out-there to believe. Each shocking oddity proves that truth is stranger than fiction. But it takes a keen eye, a sharp mind, and good instincts to spot the difference. Can you handle it?

Each Ripley's Brain Buster contains a group of four unbelievably strange statements. In each group only **one** is **false**. Read each extra-odd entry and circle whether you **Believe It!** or **Not!** And if you're up to the challenge, take on the bonus question in each section and the Pop Quiz at the end of the book. Then flip to the Answer Key, keep track of your score, and rate your skills.

Sometimes what's strangest about people isn't their odd behavior or the funny ways in which they alter their appearance—it's the human body itself. Which one of these bizarre body facts is completely false?

**a.** There are 625 sweat glands in each square inch of your skin.

**Believe It!**        **Not!**

**b.** By the time you reach the age of 70, you will have shed 40 pounds of skin.

**Believe It!**        **Not!**

**c.** Taste is the only one of the five senses with a direct connection to the brain. It's also closest to the parts of the brain that trigger memories and emotions. That's why one taste of something can bring on a flood of memories.

**Believe It!**        **Not!**

**d.** A person blinks an average of 84,000,000 times a year!

**Believe It!**        **Not!**

● ● ● ● ● ● ● ● ● ● ● ● ● ● ● ● ● ● ● ● ● ● ● ● ● ● ● ● ● ● ● ● ● ● ● ● ● ● ● ● ● ● ● ● ●

## BONUS QUESTION

**Some people will try anything! A dogmobile was patented in the United States in 1870. What did it do?**

**a.** It provided motorized transportation for dogs that could no longer walk.

**b.** It provided front-wheel drive by means of two dogs running inside a cage in the front wheels.

**c.** It used dogs instead of horses to pull small carriages.

# CHAPTER 2

# Mind Over Matter

Get ready to meet a group of people whose superhuman powers of memory, daring, or physical strength are phenomenal.

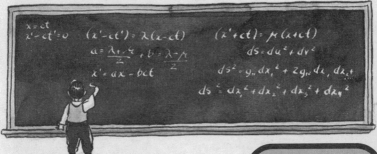

$$x = ct$$
$$x' - ct' = 0 \quad (x' - ct') = \lambda (x - ct) \quad (x' + ct) = \mu (x + ct)$$
$$a = \frac{\lambda + \mu}{2}, \, b = \frac{\lambda - \mu}{2} \quad ds = du^2 + dv^2$$
$$x' = ax - bct \quad ds^2 = g_{11} \, dx_1^2 + 2g_{12} \, dx_1 \, dx_1 +$$
$$ds^2 = dx_1^2 + dx_2^2 + dx_3^2 + dx_4^2$$

**No Problem:** At the age of four, Ung-Young Kim of Seoul, South Korea, could solve mathematical problems based on Einstein's theory of relativity.

**Baby Tape Recorder:** Murasaki Shikibu had such a remarkable memory that, at the age of two, she could repeat 1,000 lines of poetry after having heard them just once.

## Would You Believe?

At the age of five, little Louis Miller of Philadelphia . . .

**a.** got his black belt in karate.
**b.** composed his first opera.
**c.** was accepted at the University of Pennsylvania.
**d.** spoke eight languages.

**Gravely Unsettling:** Nicholas Settle of Nyack, New York, could walk through any cemetery once, then recite the epitaphs on each tombstone from memory.

**Little Professor:** Jean-Philippe Bratier (1721–1740) spoke German, French, and Latin at the age of four, translated the Greek Bible at age five, and read Hebrew at age six.

**Fully Committed:** Elijah, the Gaon, chief rabbi of Lithuania, committed 2,500 books, including the Bible and the Talmud, to memory, and could repeat any passage from them at will.

## Would You Believe?

Guy Mitchell of Iowa passed the Morse code test for his radio operator's license . . .

**a.** at the age of four.
**b.** without studying.
**c.** on his tenth birthday.
**d.** by using sign language.

**Mad Professor:** The Oxford English Dictionary was begun in London in 1878 under the editorship of Professor James Murray, who solicited entries from volunteers. One volunteer, American Army surgeon Dr. William Charles Minor, who had served in the Civil War, was responsible for about 10,000 entries. Murray was so impressed by Minor's scholarship that he repeatedly invited Minor to visit him. But Minor never accepted. The reason? He was an inmate in the Broadmoor Hospital for the Criminally Insane, where he had been confined in 1871 for killing a man while in a deluded state.

**Most Noteworthy:** Musician and composer Wolfgang Amadeus Mozart (1756–1791) could listen to a symphony by another composer once, then write it down, note for note.

**Early Learning:** English economist and philosopher John Stuart Mill learned Greek at the age of three. By the time he was eight, he also knew Latin, which he taught to his sister.

**Fun with Numbers:** Savant Paul Erdös was a brilliant mathematician, but when it came to day-to-day living, he was mentally, physically, and socially challenged. Just opening a simple container could pose a major problem for him. Once he stabbed a can of juice with a pair of scissors, spilling the contents all over the floor. Though Erdös was the most published mathematician of all time, he could not even tie his own shoelaces! Erdös rarely bathed or changed his clothes, but he was warmly welcomed by many world-class mathematicians, who were eager to bask in the light of his genius.

**Word Perfect:** Jack Fletcher of Wargrave, England, was considered the "village idiot," yet he could quote every sermon he heard in any of ten nearby churches word for word, giving a perfect imitation of each preacher's voice and delivery.

## Large Hard Drive:

The savant Kim Peek, inspiration for the film *Rain Man*, read his first book at the age of 16 months. Peek has a brain that is one-third larger than normal. Because there is no separation, or filtering mechanism, between the left and right sides of his brain, it saves every piece of information it receives.

Perhaps this is why Peek can not only tell you the day of the week for any date in history, but can also recall every word of the more than 8,000 books he's read so far.

### Would You Believe?

England's King George III (1738–1820) could recite from memory . . .

**a.** the titles of all 2,500 books in his castle library.

**b.** the 10,000 virtues required of a king.

**c.** the complete works of St. Augustine—containing eight million words.

**d.** the names of all 4,500 officers in the British Navy and the ship to which each was assigned.

**Well Balanced:** In 1953, 148-pound Bob Dotzauer balanced three lawnmowers on his chin—which, combined, weighed five pounds more than he did.

**Human Bridge:** Eighteenth-century strongman Thomas Topham of Derby, England, could lie suspended between two stools and lift a six-foot-long table with his teeth while four men stood on his body.

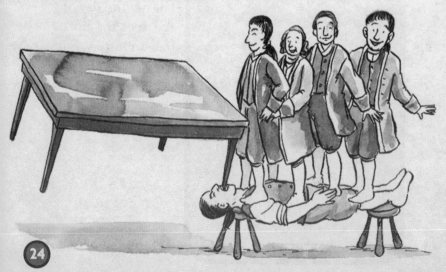

**Nice Kitty:** German circus performer Miss Heliot entertained audiences in 1953 by carrying a 660-pound lion on her shoulders.

## Would You Believe?

In 1979, John Massis of Belgium prevented a helicopter from taking off, using a rope and harness held . . .

**a.** between two fingers.
**b.** in his teeth.
**c.** around his neck.
**d.** in his clenched fists.

**Strong-arm Tactic:** Allen Durwood, bodyguard to King Malcolm McAnmore of Scotland, was so strong he was able to keep 20 assassins from entering the castle by holding the door closed with just one arm.

## Tiny Chairman:

At the age of five months, Victor Casados, Jr., could simultaneously lift two chairs weighing nine pounds each.

## Uplifting Performance:

In the 18th century, Miss Darnett, known as "The Singing Strong Lady," sang a song while supporting a platform that held the pianist and his piano.

## Supportive Husband:

In the late 1890s, famous Canadian strongman Louis Cyr supported his 125-pound wife as she climbed a ladder that he held in one outstretched hand.

**Pulling a Fast One:** Kevin Fast was nicknamed "Bench" in college because he could bench press 500 pounds. Since then, he's been inspired to try something no one's attempted before—pulling two giant fire engines. It normally takes seven men to move just one fire engine, but Fast was able to move both!

**Heavy Load:** Len Ashton, a South African circus performer, can balance heavy objects on his chin—such as a lawn mower, his three-year-old son seated on a chair, and a washing machine.

## Would You Believe?

In 1990, Malaysian strongman R. Letchemanah pulled a Boeing 737 airplane 50 feet with his . . .

**a.** right arm.
**b.** little finger.
**c.** hair.
**d.** leg.

**Hot Feat:** On August 2, 1938, people gasped in astonishment as they watched Kuda Bux of India walk through fire. A ditch 20 feet long, three feet wide, and four

feet deep outside of Radio City Music Hall in New York City had been filled with a layer of fiery coals. Twenty-four hours later, the temperature inside the pit had reached more than 1,200°F. After walking the length of the ditch through the hot coals barefoot up to his ankles, Bux was examined by doctors, who found no injuries.

**Helping Hands:** Master Zhou is an expert in a Chinese art called Tchi Gong, which uses energy to heal. The energy that flows through Zhou's hands has been recorded at 202°F. Zhou begins treatment with what looks like a simple massage. Then he wraps a piece of tin foil inside a moistened paper towel and places it on the patient's chest. As he passes his hands over it, steam rises from the paper towel. People who have had the treatment claim to feel more focused and full of energy. Others believe they have been cured of a variety of ailments from headaches to cancer.

**Suspended Animation:** In 1837, to demonstrate the power of meditation, a yogi named Haridas allowed himself to be buried alive for 40 days. In preparation for the ordeal, the mystic went into a self-induced trance. Before burying him, his assistants filled his ears, nose, and mouth with wax and wrapped him in a blanket. A guard was posted at his "grave" to make sure that no trickery took place. When the assistants dug Haridas up 40 days later, he was extremely thin but otherwise in perfect shape.

## Would You Believe?

While lying on a bed of nails, yogi Zdenek Zahradka of Ústí nad Labem, Czech Republic, regularly . . .

**a.** practiced mental telepathy.
**b.** slept.
**c.** practiced yoga.
**d.** gave blood.

**Over the Edge:** Extreme kayaker Tao Berman was the first person to go over Johnston Canyon Waterfall at Banff National Park in Alberta, Canada. Equivalent to a jump from a ten-story building, the 98-foot drop is just eight feet wide at the top and lined on both sides with jagged rocks.

**Leaps of Faith:** The Land Divers of Pentecost, one of the islands of Vanuatu in the South Pacific, have been bungee-jumping for hundreds of years—but they use vines instead of bungee cords. The divers jump headfirst from an 80-foot-high tower. The vines attached to their ankles slow their plunges, but each year, some divers are injured when the vines snap. Why do they do it? It's a coming-of-age ritual, with boys as young as eight making their first jump.

## Respect Your Elders:

On December 10, 1997, Julia "Butterfly" Hill climbed 180 feet up an ancient redwood tree in a bold attempt to save a forest from being cut down. She did not come down for two years. Enclosed in a dome of multi-colored tarps, Hill lived on a tiny wooden platform, using a bucket for a toilet, candles for light, and a one-burner propane stove to cook on.

A ground crew brought her supplies, which she pulled up with ropes. During her record-breaking time in the tree, Hill endured 90-mile-per-hour winds and harassment by lumber company helicopters. She came down only when the company agreed to protect the surrounding three acres from logging.

## Would You Believe?

Using only one finger, Mike Gooch of England performed 16 consecutive push-ups, balanced on a . . .

**a.** coconut.
**b.** merry-go-round.
**c.** seesaw.
**d.** Ping-Pong ball.

**A Wheely Great Time:** One of Canadian unicyclist Kris Holm's record-breaking stunts involved riding within four inches of a 2,000-foot cliff and leaping six feet across a crevasse thousands of feet deep—all without brakes and with nothing to hold on to.

## Would You Believe?

Nature photographer Tony Hurtubise invented a suit 50 times stronger and 85 percent lighter than steel. To test it out, he . . .

**a.** was shot out of a cannon into a brick wall.
**b.** let a train run over him.
**c.** wrestled with a grizzly bear.
**d.** had a car suspended on wires swung into his chest like a pendulum.

**Double-cross:** The Adung River Bridge in Myanmar consists only of a 150-foot-long rope strung 40 feet above the water. Women with babies strapped to their backs haul themselves across the bridge while hanging upside down in a ring made of reeds.

# Brain Buster

How fine-tuned is your radar for the ridiculous? Figure out which one of the following four amazing abilities is too blatantly false to believe.

**a.** On his 80th birthday, Master Engineer Junior Grade Gardner A. Taylor lifted a 110-pound anvil that was suspended from his ears! His set his own lifetime record at age 64 when he lifted 175 pounds using ear power alone.

**Believe It!**　　　**Not!**

**b.** In the 1930s, George Bove of New York City claimed he could determine a person's gender by dangling a key on a piece of thread over a handwriting sample. And he was right every time!

**Believe It!**　　　**Not!**

**c.** In the 1980s, Gabrielle O'Mally became a legend at Ripley's Odditoriums around the nation by spinning her left foot 360 degrees on her ankle joint.

**Believe It!**　　　**Not!**

**d.** In June 1930, U.S. Navy wrestling champion Joe Reno was hypnotized and slept buried in a coffin for almost 17 days without food or water. But nothing could keep Joe down. Only 15 minutes after being awakened and released from the coffin, Joe wrestled middleweight champion Red Lindsay for ten minutes before the match was declared a tie.

**Believe It!**　　　**Not!**

# BONUS QUESTION

**What amazing feat did Lotte Frutiger of Allalinhorn, Switzerland, accomplish in 1927 when she was only eight years old?**

**a.** She became the youngest person ever to hold the record for ice diving. She immersed herself in icy water for over 40 minutes!

**b.** She climbed Mount Allalinhorn, which is 13,234 feet high and always covered in ice.

**c.** She had herself buried alive in a block of ice and survived for 78 hours without food and water.

The following pages are filled with individuals who dare to be different in ways that most people would never even dream of.

### Cat-echism:

During the 16th century, England's Cardinal Wolsey (1475–1530) regularly took his cats to church.

### Would You Believe?

German poet Friedrich von Schiller (1759–1805) could only compose poetry while sitting . . .

**a.** with his parakeet on his head.
**b.** in his pajamas.
**c.** with his cat in his lap.
**d.** with his feet in ice water.

### Chilling Performance:

During the 1939 World's Fair, performance artist Annetta Del Mar of Chicago, Illinois, had her body entirely frozen and thawed up to 30 times a day.

**Junk Food:** Michel Lotito, long considered a medical mystery, found that his unusual ability to chew and swallow indigestible household objects such as razor blades, nuts, bolts, china, glasses, and cutlery could be parlayed into a career. To date, he has ingested a grocery cart, a bicycle, a coffin, and a complete Cessna airplane.

**Riveting Performance:** In the 1970s, Bill Steed, a professor of frog psychology at Croaker College, used hypnosis to train frogs to perform amazing feats such as lifting barbells.

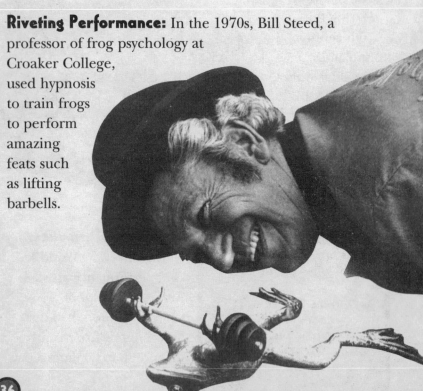

## Tummy Tuck:

Alfred Hitchcock, the famous film director of movies such as *Psycho* and *The Birds,* thought belly buttons were ugly. So he had his own surgically removed.

## Beastly Welcome:

Writer and naturalist Charles Waterton (1782–1864) sometimes slept outside with a tree-dwelling mammal called a sloth. He was also known to act like a dog, greet his guests with a growl, and scratch his head with his big toe.

### Would You Believe?

King Henry II of France suffered from ailurophobia, a terrible fear of . . .

**a.** snakes.
**b.** birds.
**c.** cats.
**d.** bees.

**Suit Sower:** One day the seed of an idea for a new act popped into performance artist Gene Pool's head. Why not grow a suit out of grass and then get chased by a lawn mower? He did just that and, in the process, discovered that he had a green thumb. Not one to let the grass grow under his feet, Pool started his own clothing line and has perfected his art to the point where he can grow an entire three-piece suit in just two weeks. Grass-covered cars are another of his specialties.

**Fowl Fashion:** During the 1700s, Ignatz Von Roll, a turkey farmer in Germany, had all of his birds fitted with tiny Turkish turbans.

**Cornball Gown:** In 1947, Virginia Winn of Mercedes, Texas, stitched 60,000 grains of corn onto an evening dress. The completed gown weighed 40 pounds.

**All the News That's Fit to Wear:** It took Mrs. Willis N. Ward and Mrs. J. Hoppemath the better part of 1939 to make their newsprint coats.

**All Buttoned Up:** In 1936, Owen Totten of Mt. Erie, Illinois, modeled a suit he'd covered with 5,600 buttons— no two of which were alike.

## Would You Believe?

Bill Black of St. Louis, Missouri, started an entire line of clothing made of . . .

**a.** ostrich feathers.
**b.** human hair.
**c.** seashells.
**d.** moss.

**A Dog's Life:** The eighth Earl of Bridgewater, who died in 1829, dressed his dogs in fine clothing and allowed them to eat dinner at his table every day.

**Gem of a Meal:** King Henry III of France, who ruled from 1574 to 1589, dined regularly on partridges coated with solid gold, omelets sprinkled with ground-up pearls, and poultry soaked in expensive perfume.

**Puppy Love:** France's King Henry III was also so fond of pets that whenever his favorite dog had a litter, he'd carry the puppies for days in a basket slung from his neck.

**Lovebirds:** To appease the gods, Khanderav, ruler of Baroda, India, from 1856 to 1870, spent $200,000 to host 42 marriage ceremonies. In each case, the bride and groom were pigeons.

**Had Their Cake and Heard It, Too:** In 1533, at the wedding of the Duke of Orléans (who became Henry II of France) and Catherine de Médicis, a four-piece orchestra played to the guests from inside a huge wedding cake.

## Would You Believe?

To improve their studies, schoolboys in Morocco are fed . . .

**a.** ground toadstools.
**b.** shark eyeballs.
**c.** salmon tails.
**d.** hedgehog livers.

## Caveman Chic:

During the 18th century, Charles Hamilton, a wealthy eccentric, paid a hermit $700 to live in a cave in his garden.

## Worth His Salt:

American millionaire Alfred Gwynne Vanderbilt was so superstitious that he slept with the legs of his bed set in dishes of salt.

**Lullaby King:** King Philip V (1683–1746) of Spain cured his insomnia by hiring opera singer Carlo Farinelli to sing him to sleep each night.

## Would You Believe?

King Louis XIV of France regularly washed only the tip of his nose because . . .

**a.** of the low water supply.
**b.** he was afraid of water.
**c.** of his religious beliefs.
**d.** he hated the taste of water.

**Wedding Costume:** Allen Roulston and Linda MacLaggan of Toronto, Canada, dressed up as Frankenstein and the Bride of Frankenstein for their Halloween Day wedding.

**Lionhearted:** French actor Charles Dullin (1885–1949) spent several years training for the stage by reciting poetry daily while inside a cage filled with lions.

## Through the Roof:

American financier J. Pierpont Morgan was so committed to wearing extra-high silk top hats that he ordered high-roofed limousines custom-built for himself.

## Fowl Balls:

In 1989, a group of grocery store clerks in Newport, California, formed an unofficial bowling league called the Poultry Association. Using frozen turkeys as bowling balls and one-liter soft-drink bottles as pins, they bowled to raise money for charity.

## Captive Audience:

The faithful widow Countess Antoinette de Bethune Pologne kept her husband's skull on her desk and read to it from his favorite two books every day for 25 years.

## Horsing Around:

In the 19th century, Jonathan James Toogood from Overblow, England, regularly jumped his horse over hedges while riding backward.

## Would You Believe?

The French poet Charles Baudelaire (1821–1867) walked through the parks of Paris . . .

**a.** wearing only his bathrobe.
**b.** with a parrot on his shoulder.
**c.** with a lobster on a leash.
**d.** with a mouse in his pocket.

**Dirty Trick:** In the 1930s in Howe, Indiana, a woman, known locally as the "Animal Woman," lived with skunks and did not bathe or change her clothes for 25 years. As if to prove the wisdom of her lifestyle, she died ten days after she was given her first bath.

**Major Tantrum:** When his parents refused to buy him a motorcycle, Dan Jaimun of Bangkok, Thailand, locked himself in his room and stayed there for 22 years.

## Señor Lancelot:

Juanito Apiñani, a 19th-century Spanish matador, thrilled crowds by using a lance to leap over charging bulls.

## Would You Believe?

Every morning before British poet Edith Sitwell began to work she . . .

**a.** took a bath in a tub of milk.
**b.** ate a dozen pancakes with jam.
**c.** lay in an open coffin.
**d.** fed her 60 pet cockatiels.

## High-tech Howard:

In 1938, millionaire Howard Hughes set a round-the-world speed record, flying at 352.39 miles per hour in a plane that was filled with Ping-Pong balls. He took the balls along so they would cushion his fall and keep him afloat in case he crashed into the ocean.

**The following people could ace a talent competition any day. Can you pick out which twisted talent is not real?**

**a.** Ruwan Jayatilleke of Englewood, New Jersey, can shoot peas out of his nose at speeds of up to 30 miles per hour.

**Believe It!**       **Not!**

**b.** At only three and a half months old, Ted Elbert Carmack could lift his own weight on a chin-up bar.

**Believe It!**       **Not!**

**c.** In the 1940s, Alan Cooke of Baltimore, Maryland, could eat, sleep, and drink while floating in water. To prove that he wouldn't sink, he was thrown tied, taped, and bound into the Chesapeake Bay 15 times, into Lake Michigan, and into various rivers and indoor pools. He floated to the surface every time!

**Believe It!**       **Not!**

**d.** On December 4, 1934, Forrest Yanky lassoed a housefly with a piece of thread while his entire family watched in awe.

**Believe It!**       **Not!**

# BONUS QUESTION

**What made poet Emily Dickinson (1830–1903) a little out of the ordinary?**

**a.** She never wrote down a single word on paper. Instead, she committed each of her poems to memory and recited them to her circle of friends.

**b.** She had a constant headache for 26 years, yet never missed a day of writing.

**c.** She thought she was so ugly, she would stay in another room whenever she had visitors and talk to them through an open door.

# CHAPTER 4 Weird Ways

**Things that seem perfectly natural to some people may seem downright strange to others.**

**Balancing Act:**
Women of the Balanta tribe in Binnar, Guinea-Bissau, Africa, annually perform a dance in which they balance a huge basket containing their sweetheart or husband on their head.

**Would You Believe?**
For a month after his wedding, an African Masai bridegroom must . . .

**a.** do all the cooking.
**b.** wear his wife's clothing.
**c.** obey his mother-in-law.
**d.** wash all the dishes.

**H$_2$O for K9s:**
A supermarket in Blackhawk, California, sells Thirsty Pup, a bottled water for dogs.

**Nature's Night-lights:** One of the world's oldest plants, the puya raimondi, grows in the Cordillera Mountains of Peru. These plants feature a shaft of blossoms that grows more than 30 feet high. The shafts are so saturated with resin that shepherds ignite them to light their way.

**Get a Grip:** Zulu mothers wear their hair in such a manner that their children can cling to it for security when riding piggyback.

**Amazon.pod:** Giant pods that protect the buds on palm trees are used by people of the Brazilian jungle as bathtubs.

**Barely Believable:** Donald Duck comic books were once banned in Finland because Donald didn't wear pants.

**Pup Power:** Nanay children in Siberia travel to and from their distant school on skis pulled by dogs.

## Would You Believe?

In ancient Rome, a bad haircut was thought to . . .

**a.** lead to baldness.
**b.** encourage violence.
**c.** turn one's hair gray.
**d.** cause storms.

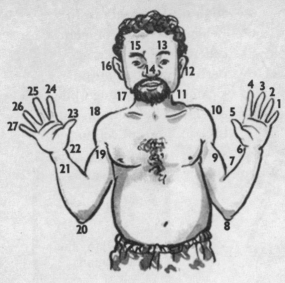

## Body Count:

Instead of counting by tens as Westerners do, the people of the Min tribe in Papua New Guinea count by 27s—not only on their fingers, but on various other body parts. They begin counting on the little finger of their left hand. Then, when they run out of fingers, they count the left wrist, forearm, elbow, biceps, shoulder, side of the neck, ear, and eye—that's 13. The bridge of the nose makes 14. Then they count the right eye, ear, side of the neck, shoulder, biceps, elbow, forearm, wrist, and five right fingers to reach a total of 27.

## Just Spit It Out:

It's considered good manners in Kenya for Masai warriors to spit at each other when they meet.

**High on Themselves:** In Belgium, a group of men called Les Echassiers perform combat moves, kicking and hopping while on stilts. The tradition dates back to the 15th century.

**Would You Believe?**

Men in Romania once had to obtain a government permit to . . .

**a.** walk barefoot.
**b.** carry an umbrella.
**c.** shave their beards.
**d.** grow a beard.

**Leaf Luge:** Instead of using sleds, the Iraku children of Africa slide down mountainsides on large cactus leaves.

**Knee-On Lights:** In Israel's Negev Desert, camels are required to wear reflectors on their knees at night.

## Earth Tones:

In Caryville, Florida, there is an annual International Worm Fiddling contest in which contestants play music to draw earthworms out of the soil.

## Crop Raising:

To protect their vegetables from ants and animals, indigenous people in the Orinoco forests of South America plant their crops in boats set on frames high above the ground.

**Sea Scrawlers:** Sea urchin spines, which can reach six inches long, are used as pencils by schoolchildren on the Pacific island of Rarotonga.

**Totem Calls:** In the South Pacific islands of Vanuatu, trees are carved and hollowed out to make huge, resonant drums that are used for interisland communication.

**On Pins and Needles:** A popular amusement among the rural population of Bohemia in the Czech Republic is an annual pin-sticking contest to determine the best human pincushion. In 1928, the king of a Gypsy tribe won the contest by enduring 3,200 needles in his arm for a period of 31 hours. His record has never been broken.

## Would You Believe?

The Yoruba people of Africa must give a gift to every woman they pass who is . . .

**a.** engaged.
**b.** holding twins.
**c.** in mourning.
**d.** a newlywed.

## Fee, Fi, Fo, Fum:

A type of bean pod found in Myanmar grows to a height of four feet and is so sturdy that the Arakanese use it as a stairway to their dwellings.

## Grin and Bear It:

In Romania, some people believed that a man suffering from rheumatism could recover his health by having a trained bear walk on his back for half an hour.

**Sticky Situation:** Once a year, the children of Ravensburg, Germany, march through the streets swinging long branches in memory of the bubonic plague in the 14th century. At the time of the plague, people were so afraid of catching the disease, they waved long sticks at one another instead of shaking hands.

**Juicy Jewelry:**
In New Guinea, sago-maggots are worn as jewelry but can also serve as a snack for hungry travelers.

# For Beauty's Sake

Beauty can come in a variety of shapes and sizes.

**A Heady Experience:** The Mangbetu of Africa once bound infants' heads to elongate the skull. To accent their beauty, both men and women wrapped their hair around baskets.

**High Necklines:** Swanlike necks, a sign of beauty among the Padaung people (above) of Thailand, are achieved through the gradual addition of necklace rings.

**On File:** Renda Long of Glendale, Arizona, has not cut her nails since 1974. No wonder she prefers clothes without buttons!

**Stuck Up:** The 1990s brought us this cutting edge fashion. For some, nose and tongue piercing are still all the rage.

# Making Faces

Some people see their faces as lumps of clay to be reshaped and adorned.

**Blue in the Face:** Omi (above) appeared in Ripley's New York City Odditorium in 1940. Can you guess what his favorite color was?

**Lizard of Oddities:** Eric Sprague's (left) love of reptiles has prompted him to do his best to look like one.

**Two-Faced:** Elizabeth Christensen has always felt that she was the reincarnation of the Egyptian Queen Nefertiti. After undergoing 240 operations, she now believes she looks like her as well.

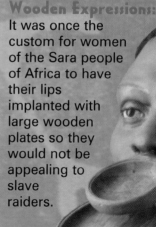

**Wooden Expressions:** It was once the custom for women of the Sara people of Africa to have their lips implanted with large wooden plates so they would not be appealing to slave raiders.

**Purr-fect:** Jocelyne Wildenstein aspired to look like a cat. Many surgeries later, it seems she has achieved her goal.

# ODDITORIUM
## FAVORITES

Many people seem as odd-inary now as when Robert Ripley first brought them to the public's attention.

**A Bright Idea:** "Lighthouse Man" used his head as a candlestick in the 1920s.

**What a Kick:** In the 1930s, Francesco Lentini of Sicily, Italy, was a master musician. He was also a renowned soccer player. Perhaps having three legs contributed to his success on the field!

**Pop-Eyes:** Avelino Perez Matos (right) of Cuba could pop his eyeballs in and out of their sockets.

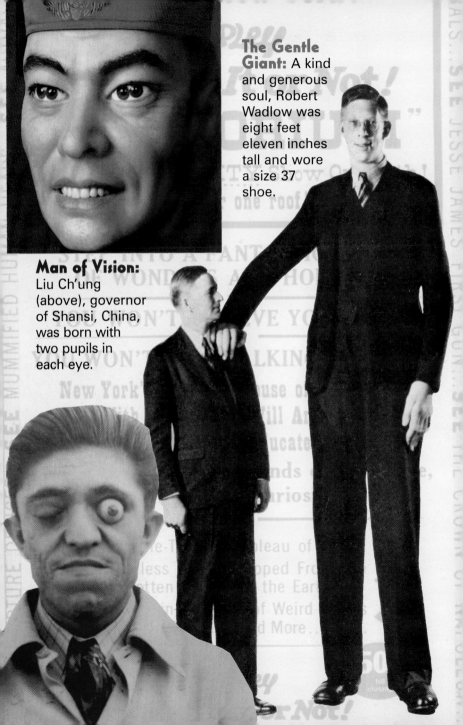

**The Gentle Giant:** A kind and generous soul, Robert Wadlow was eight feet eleven inches tall and wore a size 37 shoe.

**Man of Vision:** Liu Ch'ung (above), governor of Shansi, China, was born with two pupils in each eye.

# Some people will do anything

## What goes in . . .

**Eyestrain:** In 1933, Mr. McGregor led Mrs. McGregor around with his eyelids.

**Airhead:** We all have our talents. One of Alfred Langevin's was blowing up a balloon by expelling air through his eye.

## . . . must come out!

Dagmar Rothman could swallow an entire mouse—and bring the critter up from his stomach unharmed!

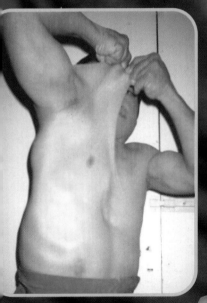

**Rubber-Necker:** Contortionist Thomas Martin Peres, also known as "Mr. Stretch," loves to shock people by pulling the skin from his neck up over his nose like a turtleneck sweater.

**Feeling No Pain:** During his Painless Wonder act, Leo Kongee sewed buttons to his tongue and drove nails into his nose without feeling a twinge.

A woman's power to achieve her goals knows no bounds.

# SUPERWOMEN

**All Pumped Up:** Valentina Chepiga trained with weights to sculpt her body into such fantastic shape, she won the title of Ms. Olympia bodybuilding champion.

**Up a Tree:** Julia "Butterfly" Hill (above) would do anything to save the forest she loves so much—including living 180 feet up in an ancient redwood tree for two years.

**Power Trip:** You can count on teenager Shannon Pole Summer (right) to pull her own weight and much, much more—like a truck filled with football players, a combined weight of 12,720 pounds!

**Trick or Treat:** In the United States, a company makes InsectNside— amber-colored candies that are filled with real bugs. *Bon appétit!*

**A Hot Time:** Medieval monks created primitive alarm clocks by placing a lit candle between their toes. When the flame singed their skin, they knew it was time to rise and shine.

## Would You Believe?

It was once against the law in Indiana to kiss someone if you had . . .

**a.** a beard.
**b.** pierced ears.
**c.** influenza.
**d.** poison ivy.

**Royal Shock Absorbers:** In Germany during the 19th century, every prince had a *purgelknaben,* a boy who was raised with the young prince and spanked whenever the prince misbehaved.

**Snakes in the Grass:** Female snake-worshipers of Dahomey, Africa, are obliged to pick up every snake they encounter and transport it to the nearest temple— wearing it like a necklace!

## Would You Believe?

The polite way to greet someone in Tibet is to . . .

**a.** kick stones out of his or her path.

**b.** hand him or her a piece of fresh fruit.

**c.** bow and stick out your tongue three times.

**d.** yodel.

**Check out the following four fantastic human abilities and figure out which one is completely made up.**

**a.** In 1935, El Gran Lazaro of Havana, Cuba, put a needle in his eye socket and pulled it out of his mouth!
**Believe It!**          **Not!**

**b.** Twelve-year-old Matthew Jenkins of Omaha, Nebraska, can catch and eat flies with his tongue. He says they taste like crunchy raisins.
**Believe It!**          **Not!**

**c.** It took Jedediah Buxton one month to figure out that someone could fit 586,040,972,673,024,000 human hairs into one cubic mile.
**Believe It!**          **Not!**

**d.** Jim Purol can stuff 151 drinking straws into his mouth.
**Believe It!**          **Not!**

## BONUS QUESTION

When the people in Yamanakako, Japan, get stressed out, they have a special way of relieving tension. What do they do?

**a.** They rent megaphones and scream at the top of their lungs until they shatter all the glass in their immediate vicinity.

**b.** They rent "relief rooms" where they can take their frustrations out by smashing reproductions of antiques.

**c.** They put on special foam rubber suits and rent "rubber rooms" where they can fling themselves at the walls and bounce off without getting injured.

Everyone has his or her own natural abilities and strengths. It's just that some seem more unnatural than others.

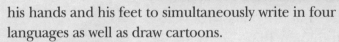

**Sketchy Stunt:** In 1934, Tom Breen of New York used both his hands and his feet to simultaneously write in four languages as well as draw cartoons.

## Would You Believe?

What United States president could simultaneously write in Latin with one hand and in Greek with the other?

**a.** James A. Garfield.
**b.** Dwight D. Eisenhower.
**c.** Richard M. Nixon.
**d.** Franklin D. Roosevelt.

**Suspension of Disbelief:** Members of the Texas-based Traumatic Stress Discipline Club are hooked on having themselves hoisted into the air by ropes, cables, and pulleys that are attached to hooks pierced through their skin (*see color insert*).

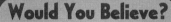

**Pressing Engagement:** Using pain-deadening meditation, Tim Cridland can lie on a bed of nails and allow a 3,000-pound vehicle to drive over him.

**Human Pincushion:** A featured performer at the Dallas, Texas, Odditorium in 1937, A. Bryant would stick up to a hundred pins and needles into his body at one time.

**Head Trip:** In 1931, entertainer Alexandre Patty bounced up and down a flight of stairs on his head.

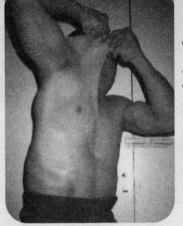

**Thin Skin:** Las Vegas contortionist and performer Thomas Martin Peres, also known as "Mr. Stretch," loves to shock people by pulling the skin of his neck up over his nose like a turtleneck sweater.

**Tongue Depressor:** In 1938, Leona Young of Norwich, New York, astounded audiences with her ability to withstand the heat of a plumber's blowtorch on her tongue—earning her the nickname the "Devil's Daughter."

## Would You Believe?

New members are admitted to the Bird Men, a secret society of acrobatic dancers in Guinea, Africa, only if they can . . .

**a.** stand on their head.
**b.** walk on their hands.
**c.** hop on one hand.
**d.** swivel their head 180 degrees.

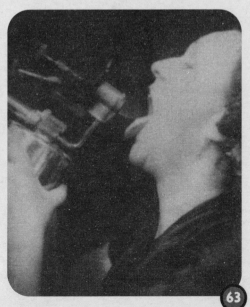

## The Write Stuff:

In 1942, Lena Deeter of Conway, Arkansas, amazed audiences by showing them how she could simultaneously write with both hands in different directions.

## Birdcalls:

Elie Gourbeyre of Nouara, France, could lure any bird to her shoulder merely by crooking her finger. This strange talent lasted only from the time she was six until she was 12 years old.

## Painless in Pittsburgh:

Leo Kongee (*see color insert*) of Pittsburgh, Pennsylvania, could drive nails into his nose, use thumbtacks to hold up his socks, and sew buttons onto his tongue without feeling any pain.

## Would You Believe?

The Mayoruna people of Brazil insert eight-inch-long palm spines through their noses and lips and tattoo whiskers on their faces because they believe they are descended from . . .

**a.** mountain lions.
**b.** tigers.
**c.** rats.
**d.** panthers.

**By the Skin of Her Teeth:** In 1934, aerialist Tiny Kline glided across Times Square 100 feet off the ground—while hanging by her mouth! She was fitted with a special mouthpiece attached to a pulley for the stunt.

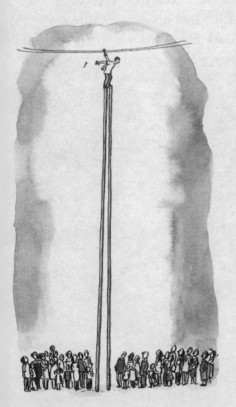

**Stiff Competition:** Not everyone is tall, but there are other ways to reach new heights. Meet the Wolf family. For ten years, Edward Wolf held the record for walking on the tallest pair of stilts ever—40 feet 9.5 inches to be exact. Then in 1998, his son Travis broke that record by walking on stilts that were 40 feet 10.25 inches high. Travis hopes he'll keep his title a long time, but the odds are getting smaller since siblings Ashley, Tony, and Jordan are well on their way to catching up with him.

### Rubber Face:
J. T. Saylors of Memphis, Tennessee, was able to "swallow" his nose.

### On Bended Knee:
In the 1930s, F. Velez Campos of Puerto Rico had his own unique way of kneeling down.

## Would You Believe?

Vaudeville contortionist King Brawn could fit his entire body . . .

**a.** into a balloon.
**b.** through a tennis racket.
**c.** through a basketball hoop.
**d.** into a clothes dryer.

## Human Owl:

Martin Joe Laurello drew large crowds to Ripley's Odditoriums throughout the 1930s. His ability to swivel his head 180 degrees never failed to amaze audiences.

**All Bottled Up:** Hugo Zamarate of Argentina is five feet nine inches tall, but he can fold his body to fit into a bottle that's only 26 inches high and 18 inches wide.

**Head Case:** In the 1930s, Lorraine Chevalier of Philadelphia, Pennsylvania, could sit on her own head. The famous Chevalier family of acrobats claimed that only one person was born into their family every 200 years who was capable of attaining this position.

**Thick Skin:** H. H. Getty of Edmonton, Alberta, Canada, discovered that a lit match held to his skin caused neither pain nor blistering. Though Getty visited several prominent physicians, no explanation was ever found.

## It's the Buzz!

In ancient Greece, women wore live cicadas leashed to golden thread as ornaments for their hair.

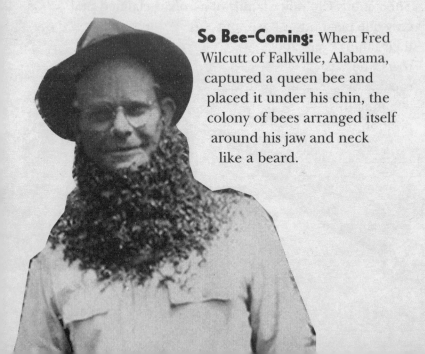

**So Bee-Coming:** When Fred Wilcutt of Falkville, Alabama, captured a queen bee and placed it under his chin, the colony of bees arranged itself around his jaw and neck like a beard.

**Nosing Around:**

In 1934, Joe Horowitz of Los Angeles, California, known as "The Man with the Iron Nose," balanced an 18-pound sword on the tip of his nose. He could perform the same feat with a lighted torch.

## Would You Believe?

In 1919, British circus performer Edith Clifford swallowed a . . .

**a.** 23-inch bayonet that was fired from a cannon.
**b.** lightbulb.
**c.** lit torch.
**d.** double-edged sword.

**Handy Trick:** In 1940, Blanche Lowe, a waitress at Clayton's Café in Tyler, Texas, could carry 23 coffee cups in one hand.

## Would You Believe?

Jim Chicon can inhale milk through one of his nostrils and spray it out from . . .

**a.** one of his ears.
**b.** his mouth.
**c.** his other nostril.
**d.** one of his eyes.

**The Unvarnished Truth:** In the 1940s, Joe Jirgles of Grand Rapids, Michigan, could hold a one-gallon can of varnish between his shoulder blades. He could also use his shoulder blades to attach himself to a fence so firmly that he could hang in place.

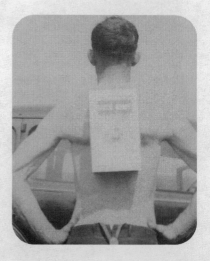

## Quick Change Artist:

In 1933, Max Calvin of Brooklyn, New York, never had to fish for change. He could hold 25 quarters in his ear.

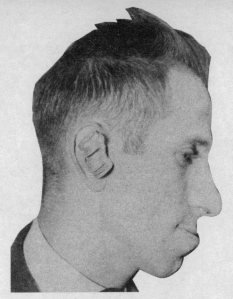

## Popping Out for a Moment:

Avelino Perez Matos of Cuba could amaze people by popping his eyeballs in and out of their sockets (*see color insert*).

## Sight for Sore Eyes:

In 1933, Odditorium performer Harry McGregor used his eyelids to pull a wagon carrying his wife.

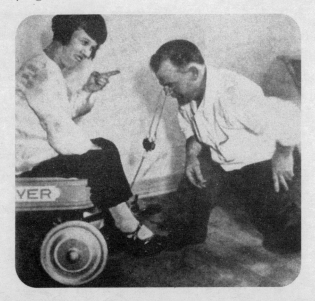

## Tale End:

C. J. Anderson wrote all his correspondence upside down and backward.

### Would You Believe?

In the 1890s, vaudeville performer William Leroy could extract large spikes from a two-inch plank using only . . .

**a.** his teeth.
**b.** his fingers.
**c.** his toes.
**d.** tweezers.

## You know what you have to do—find the fiction!

**a.** In November 1989, Polly Ketron arranged and attended her own funeral. She celebrated her 76th birthday two days later.

**Believe It!**          **Not!**

**b.** Erik Soderberg of Pittsburgh, Pennsylvania, had the lyrics of the Pokémon theme song tattooed on the inside of his lower lip.

**Believe It!**          **Not!**

**c.** Sy Bondy of Miami, Florida, collects a penny from every person he meets. Within one two-month period, he collected five million pennies or $50,000 in cash!

**Believe It!**          **Not!**

**d.** For a period of 23 years, Arthur E. Gehrke of Watertown, Wisconsin, hibernated by staying in bed each winter from Thanksgiving until Easter.

**Believe It!**          **Not!**

# BONUS QUESTION

**According to an article published by the *Toronto Star* in 1998, what was so unusual about the theft of a cement frog from the garden of John and Gertrude Knight in Swansea, Massachusetts?**

**a.** This garden decoration was valued at over $200,000,000!

**b.** The "frog-nappers" sent anonymous cards and letters to the owners from all over the world detailing the frog's exploits, then returned the garden decoration months later.

**c.** The teenagers who "borrowed" the Knights' cement frog made a digital mini-movie in which the frog skateboarded off the roof of the Knights' house, did a double back flip, and landed right back in the garden—unassisted. The Knights would never have known except that one of the filmmakers sent the video to the couple from an e-mail address that included his own last name.

## POP QUIZ

It's not over yet. How much do you remember about the oddest of the odd? It's time to find out. Circle your answers and give yourself five points for each question you answer correctly.

**1.** You wouldn't believe the things people eat. Or would you? Which of these crazy cuisine facts is *not* true?
**a.** King Henry III of France dined on partridges coated with gold and poultry soaked in perfume.
**b.** In the British countryside, shepherds drink the milk and blood of sheep for good luck—but they never eat the meat!
**c.** In New Guinea, people snack on sago maggots. YUM!

**2.** Which of the following oddities is so *not* true?
**a.** Pierre Messie of France was born with an extra nostril.
**b.** Francesco Lentini of Sicily was born with three legs.
**c.** Liu Ch'ung of China was born with two pupils in each eye.

**3.** Susan E. Weiss, of West Hempstead, New York, was born with a full set of teeth in her mouth!
      **Believe It!**        **Not!**

**4.** Which of the following was considered beautiful by fashionable women in Japan during the Middle Ages?
**a.** Elongated necks.
**b.** Stretched earlobes.
**c.** Blackened teeth.

**5.** Which of the following sensational surgeries has *not* actually been performed?

**a.** Performance artist Auralest had a third ear attached.

**b.** Alfred Hitchcock had his navel removed.

**c.** The "Bride of Wildenstein" had surgery to make her look like a cat.

**6.** At the age of two, baby Murasaki Shikibu could . . .

**a.** repeat 1,000 lines of poetry she had heard only once.

**b.** jump rope for five hours straight.

**c.** determine the pH level of a substance just by looking at it.

**7.** People are strange, and then they get stranger. Michel Lotito mystifies friends and strangers by . . .

**a.** freezing and thawing his body up to 30 times a day.

**b.** chewing and swallowing razor blades, bolts, glasses, and bicycles.

**c.** designing sportswear made out of soybeans and tofu.

**8.** Which one of the following feats is *so* amazingly false?

**a.** German circus performer Miss Heliot carried a 660-pound lion on her shoulders.

**b.** Every year, Balanta women in Guinea Bissau, Africa, perform a dance while balancing a basket holding their husband or sweetheart on their head.

**c.** Susan Dae of Tampa, Florida, subdued a runaway tiger with her bare hands and returned it to the nearby zoo without sustaining any injuries.

**9.** **What's so special about Professor Bill Steed?**
**a.** He studies frog psychology at Croaker College and uses hypnosis to train frogs to perform amazing feats like lifting barbells.
**b.** He studies the saliva of Komodo dragons in an attempt to find an antidote for biological warfare. Why? These reptiles are immune to each other's poison, and the secret to this amazing property could save lives.
**c.** He trains roaches to perform in a minicircus. With cues from a high-pitched whistle, he can make them walk on a tightrope, swing on the trapeze, and jump through flaming hoops.

**10.** **Hard to believe, but only one of the following rare royal behaviors is *not* true. Can you figure out which one?**
**a.** The eighth Earl of Bridgewater dressed his dogs in fine clothing and let them eat dinner at his table every day.
**b.** Whenever his favorite dog had puppies, King Henry III of France carried the litter in a basket slung from his neck for days.
**c.** Queen Isabella of Spain used her dog to judge the trustworthiness of visitors to the court. If the dog growled, the visitor was immediately banished to the New World.

**11.** Which of the following is completely false?
**a.** Elementary school kids in Patzcuaro, Mexico, trained an elephant to pick up a watering can, wet down the walls of their school, then wipe them down with a large brush.
**b.** Schoolchildren on the Pacific Island of Rarotonga use the spines of sea urchins as pencils. Each spine is about six inches long.
**c.** Nanay children in Siberia travel to and from their distant school on skis pulled by dogs.

**12.** Masai warriors in Kenya spit at each other when they meet—and it's considered good manners!

### Believe It!          Not!

**13.** Leo Kongee of Pittsburgh felt no pain—he drove nails into his nose, used thumbtacks to hold up his socks, and sewed buttons onto his tongue.

### Believe It!          Not!

**14.** Super Strong. Super Strange. Performer Harry McGregor was extraordinary because he could pull which of the following?
**a.** A pick-up truck filled with his entire high school marching band—a combined weight of 12,720 pounds!
**b.** His wife in a wagon using only his eyelids.
**c.** A parade float carrying the entire U.S. Olympic wrestling team, using only one arm.

**15.** Fourteen-year-old Arnold Ariello can sneeze with his eyes open. If his eyes pop out he just pushes them right back in.

### Believe It!          Not!

# Answer Key

## Chapter 1

### Would You Believe?

Page 5:  **b.** nose.

Page 6:  **c.** only half a body.

Page 9:  **a.** beards.

Page 11:  **c.** a hairy 18-inch-long mane.

Page 13:  **c.** seven feet eight inches.

Page 15:  **d.** six fingers on each hand.

Page 16:  **a.** support the three-foot-tall hairstyles of the day.

**Brain Buster:** c. is false.

**Bonus Question:** b.

## Chapter 2

### Would You Believe?

Page 19:  **c.** was accepted at the University of Pennsylvania.

Page 20:  **a.** at the age of four.

Page 23:  **d.** the names of all 4,500 officers in the British Navy and the ship to which each was assigned.

Page 25:  **b.** in his teeth.

Page 27:  **c.** hair.

Page 29:  **d.** gave blood.

Page 31:  **a.** coconut.

Page 32:  **d.** had a car suspended on wires swung into his chest like a pendulum.

**Brain Buster:** c. is false.

**Bonus Question:** b.

# Chapter 3

## Would You Believe?

Page 35: **d.** with his feet in ice water.

Page 37: **c.** cats.

Page 39: **b.** human hair.

Page 41: **d.** hedgehog livers.

Page 42: **b.** he was afraid of water.

Page 45: **c.** with a lobster on a leash.

Page 46: **c.** lay in an open coffin.

**Brain Buster:** **a.** is false.

**Bonus Question:** c.

# Chapter 4

## Would You Believe?

Page 49: **b.** wear his wife's clothing.

Page 50: **d.** cause storms.

Page 52: **d.** grow a beard.

Page 54: **b.** holding twins.

Page 57: **a.** a beard.

Page 58: **c.** bow and stick out your tongue three times.

**Brain Buster:** **b.** is false.

**Bonus Question:** b.

# Chapter 5

## Would You Believe?

Page 61:  **a.** James A. Garfield.
Page 63:  **d.** swivel their head 180 degrees.
Page 64:  **c.** rats.
Page 66:  **b.** through a tennis racket.
Page 69:  **a.** 23-inch bayonet that was fired from a cannon.
Page 70:  **d.** one of his eyes.
Page 72:  **a.** his teeth.
**Brain Buster:** **b.** is false.
**Bonus Question:** b.

## Pop Quiz

1.  **b.**
2.  **a.**
3.  **Not!**
4.  **c.**
5.  **a.**
6.  **a.**
7.  **b.**
8.  **c.**
9.  **a.**
10.  **c.**
11.  **a.**
12.  **Believe It!**
13.  **Believe It!**
14.  **b.**
15.  **Not!**

# What's Your Ripley's Rank?

# Ripley's Scorecard

**Congrats!** You've busted your brain over some of the oddest human behavior in the world and proven your ability to tell fact from fiction. Now it's time to rate your Ripley's knowledge. Are you are an Extreme Oddball or *So* Ordinary? Check out the answers in the answer key and use this page to keep track of how many trivia questions you've answered correctly. Then add 'em up and find out how you rate.

## Here's the scoring breakdown—give yourself:

★ **10 points** for every **Would You Believe?** you answered correctly;

★ **20 points** for every fiction you spotted in the **Ripley's Brain Busters**;

★ **10** for every **Bonus Question** you answered right;

★ and **5** for every **Pop Quiz** question you answered correctly.

## Here's a tally sheet:

Number of **Would You Believe?** _____ x 5  = _____
questions answered correctly:

Number of **Ripley's Brain Buster** _____ x 10 = _____
questions answered correctly:

Number of **Bonus Questions** _____ x 5  = _____
answered correctly:

Chapter Total:  _____

Write your totals for each chapter and the Pop Quiz section in the spaces below. Then add them up to get your FINAL SCORE. Your FINAL SCORE decides how you rate:

Chapter 1 Total: _____

Chapter 2 Total: _____

Chapter 3 Total _____

Chapter 4 Total: _____

Chapter 5 Total: _____

Pop Quiz Total: _____

FINAL SCORE: _____

# 525–301
## Extreme Oddball

You can't be fooled. You are fully aware of how strange the truth is and how odd human behavior can be. Your skill for spotting tall tales is beyond belief. Your brain never busts—even on the toughest Brain Busters. You amaze your friends and awe your family with your knowledge of the unusual, the unbelievable, and the just plain wacky. Perhaps your superskills will land you in the Ripley's files—you're already unbelievably amazing! Believe It!

# 300–201
## Oddly Talented

Your talent for the twisted is top-notch, and you're not afraid who knows it. Why obsess over the mundane when you can focus on the fantastic? A man who lifts weights with his ear, a woman who lifts lions—bring it on! Sometimes you get stuck on a superhard Brain Buster, but let's face it, there's always room for improvement. Overall, your ability to tell fact from fiction is out of the ordinary. Trust your instincts and go, go, go!

# 200–101
## Odd One Out

Your radar for the ridiculous is more than a little off-kilter—but you're not giving up anytime soon. You've got the basics of finding the fiction among the facts down, but you need practice on the more challenging stuff. Stories about people sticking needles in their eyes or surgically removing their belly buttons are just too bizarre for your taste. That works. Just remember, sometimes the truth is truly more bizarre than fiction.

# 100–0
## So Ordinary

The odds are against you in this game. Tales that would freak out or amaze your friends are simply humdrum and ho-hum in your world. Maybe your everyday life is wackier than the weirdest Ripley's oddity or perhaps you have better things to do with your time. Whatever the case, separating the true from the false is just not your thing. That's okay. But consider yourself warned—people are strange, and the truth is even stranger!

# Photo Credits

Ripley Entertainment Inc. and the editors of this book wish to thank the following photographers, agents, and other individuals for permission to use and reprint the following photographs in this book. Any photographs included in this book that are not acknowledged below are property of the Ripley Archives. Great effort has been made to obtain permission from the owners of all materials included in this book. Any errors that may have been made are unintentional and will gladly be corrected in future printings if notice is sent to Ripley Entertainment Inc., 5728 Major Boulevard, Orlando, Florida 32819.

## Black & White Photos

14 Padaung Girl/CORBIS

21 Wolfgang Amadeus Mozart/Library of Congress, Prints and Photographs Division, Detroit Publishing Company Collection

22 Paul Erdős/by George Csicsery from his documentary film *N Is a Number: A Portrait of Paul Erdős* (1993)

31 Julia Butterfly Hill/Shaun Walker/ ottermedia.com

32 Kris Holm/Ryan Leach

37 Alfred Hitchcock/Photo Raymond Voinquel © Ministère de la Culture, France

38 Gene Pool/Gary Sutton

44 J. Pierpont Morgan/Bettmann/CORBIS

51 Masai Warriors/Steven Drummond

54 Sea Urchin/CORBIS

57 InsectNside/Courtest of HotLix

## Color Insert

Padaung Woman and Child/CORBIS

Nobosodrou, a Mangbetu Woman in the Belgian Congo (now the Democratic Republic of the Congo)/Photograph by Léon Poirier and Georges Specht during the French Citroën Expedition through Africa, March 1925/ Postcard Collection, Eliot Elisofon Photographic Archives, National Museum of African Art, Smithsonian Institution

Young Woman with Pierced Tongue/CORBIS

Eric Sprague/Courtesy of Eric Sprague

Elizabeth Christensen/Atlantic Syndication Partners

Jocelyne Wildenstein/Andrea Renault/Globe Photos

Julia Butterfly Hill/Shaun Walker/ ottermedia.com

Valentina Chepiga/Bill Dobbins/ billdobbins.com

If you enjoyed **Odd-inary People**, you won't want to miss

 # Amazing Escapes

## In this thrilling collection of survival stories, you'll read about . . .

A golfer who finished his game after being struck by lightning

A man who was saved from execution by an earthquake— six times

A woman who saved her pet terrier's life by biting a pit bull

A fire that was extinguished by pickle juice

**Amazing Escapes** is filled with shocking stories like these—each one more outrageous than the next! So if amazing rescues and close calls are your thing, fasten your seat belt, hold on tight, and get ready for the ride of your life!

**Don't miss these other exciting**

**books . . .**

## World's Weirdest Critters

Did you know that hippo sweat looks like blood? Or that a tiger's roar can be heard up to two miles away? That golden eagles will attack planes that fly too close to their nests? You'll find these incredible creatures and tons more in the pages of **World's Weirdest Critters**.

## Creepy Stuff

How can people predict events before they actually happen? Why do the ghosts of long-dead people haunt the homes they once lived in? Why are some possessions associated with bad luck? Read about these things and more in **Creepy Stuff**. But be warned: Don't read this book before you go to sleep if you're afraid of things that go bump in the night!